Todd Goes for the Goal

Read other titles in the series

A Champion Sports Story

Batting Ninth

Library Ed. ISBN 978-0-7660-3886-8
Paperback ISBN 978-1-4644-0001-8

Matty in the Goal

Library Ed. ISBN 978-0-7660-3877-6
Paperback ISBN 978-1-4644-0003-2

Rounding Third, Heading Home!

Library Ed. ISBN 978-0-7660-3876-9
Paperback ISBN 978-1-4644-0002-5

Tony's Last Touchdown

Library Ed. ISBN 978-0-7660-3885-1
Paperback ISBN 978-1-4644-0004-9

A CHAMPION SPORTS STORY

Todd Goes for the Goal

Stuart A.P. Murray

Enslow Publishers, Inc.
40 Industrial Road
Box 398
Berkeley Heights, NJ 07922
USA

http://www.enslow.com

This book is a work of fiction. References to real people, events, establishments,
organizations, or locales are intended only to provide a sense of authenticity and
are used to advance the fictional narrative. All other characters, and all incidents and
dialogue, are drawn from the author's imagination and are not to be construed as real.

Library of Congress Cataloging-in-Publication Data

    Murray, Stuart, 1948–
      Todd goes for the goal / Stuart A.P. Murray.
         p. cm. — (A Champion sports story)
      Summary: Freshman Todd gets to try out for the varsity soccer team that his
best friend plays for, but when two junior teammates bully Todd and he moves to a
rival school, he is forced to confront the bullies—and play against his best friend.
      ISBN 978-0-7660-3887-5
      [1. Soccer—Fiction. 2. Bullies—Fiction. 3. High schools—Fiction. 4. Schools—
Fiction.] I. Title.
      PZ7.M9658To 2012
      [Fic]—dc23

                             2011022147

Paperback ISBN 978-1-4644-0000-1

ePUB ISBN 978-1-4645-0451-8

PDF ISBN 978-1-4646-0451-5

Printed in the United States of America

092011 Lake Book Manufacturing, Inc., Melrose Park, IL

10 9 8 7 6 5 4 3 2 1

Cover Illustration: © 2011 Photos.com, a division of Getty Images.

 CONTENTS

CHAPTER ONE

"Dream on, Pelé"

"Coach wants me on varsity?"

Todd Benson couldn't believe what his friend had just told him.

"That's right, dude," said Will Weatherly as the two of them walked down Elm Street, each carrying a soccer ball. "Coach said to tell you, be at practice tomorrow."

Will grinned and punched Todd in the shoulder. Will was a hefty six-foot-two junior and Todd a five-ten skinny freshman. So Todd felt that punch. It didn't matter, of course, because Will was his best friend. That was why Coach Jaynes had Will deliver the message to Todd. Will was also the team leader.

Todd and Will both loved soccer and played whenever they could—like they were going to now, on a sunny Saturday afternoon in early October. Even though they were in the middle of their high school season, they were heading to the soccer field to kick the ball and work out on their own. For one thing, Will was trying to lose weight. He wanted to get in shape, and playing goalie didn't give him much chance to run.

As they walked, Will said Coach Jaynes had arranged for Todd to change teams, junior varsity to varsity. Todd had never expected that.

"Why wouldn't he want you on the squad?" Will asked. "We aren't scoring enough, and you're on fire! How many you got already?"

Todd shrugged. He had nine goals on the jayvee team.

"But," Todd said, "it's not exactly like playing striker on varsity."

"Gadzooks!" Will exclaimed—he liked using wacky phrases. "Look how you score against the varsity when we scrimmage you jayvees!"

"Yeah, but—"

"At least you score when I'm not in goal!" Will grinned, meaning Todd sometimes scored against the backup varsity goalie.

"Yeah, well you're just lucky is all." Todd gave Will a shove and shouted, "Let's go, slowpoke!" And he took off, running, leaving Will behind.

"Hey," Will called out, "who are you trying to impress?"

Soon they were at the Highfield High School soccer field, next to the football stadium. Todd was so excited to move up to varsity that he started doing wind sprints. Will came alongside, puffing.

"Ye gods! Slow down or you'll pull a muscle." Will started to stretch. "Gotta warm up first."

Will was right, as usual. Todd admired Will, who was almost three years older. He was not only a great athlete but also a top student, especially in English and literature. That was where he got those "gadzooks" and "forsooths," another favorite of his.

Todd would have to keep his cool going up to the varsity team. The training was a lot more serious than on jayvee. He'd have to be ready, and a pulled muscle now wouldn't help.

After stretching, the two of them trotted around the field, passing a ball back and forth. Will wanted to get in shape so that as a senior next year, he'd be at his very best. He hoped to impress college scouts and earn a scholarship. He had a single mom, and there wasn't much money to pay for college. Even this year, Will hoped Highfield would do well at the state level so that he'd be noticed. Although he was only a junior, Todd was sure that Will would impress the scouts.

They stopped at one of the goals, where Todd began crossing the ball, and Will jumped to catch it. Then Todd took shots. Will rolled the ball out to him, and Todd hit it first time. Very little got past Will, though—at least on the ground.

Being a bit overweight, Will sometimes had trouble getting up to high balls. But his skill and strength made up for his poor jumping ability. He could throw and drop-kick the ball more than half field, and there was nobody braver when it came to diving into a crowd to get the ball.

Todd had good skills of his own. He could put the ball wherever he wanted to on goal. Normal shots didn't get by Will. But when Todd lofted it far into the opposite corner, Will couldn't always jump up to save it. When Will did get that high ball, it was always a great play.

Then Todd would tease him with, "Not next time, Lucky."

"Dream on, Pelé," Will would answer.

Todd noticed a few girls carrying tennis rackets passing by the field. He recognized Melanie Weatherly, her blond ponytail bobbing, and that beautiful smile—a smile surprisingly aimed at him just then! She even waved.

Todd's heart leaped. He started to wave back, but then the ball thumped him in the stomach, and he gasped.

"Pay attention, Pelé!" Will laughed.

Todd ripped back a shot, harder than he'd ever hit a ball before. Will took it full on his chest, falling backward as the ball bounced over him and into the goal.

"Odds bodkins!" Will groaned.

"Oh!" Todd gasped. "Sorry, man, you okay?"

Will sat up, half grinning, half scowling. The girls were clapping and laughing, but Todd was too shy to look that way now. Melanie was Will's cousin, a freshman like Todd, and the best-looking girl in school.

"Aha!" Will said, waving to them from where he sat. "Now I see who you're trying to impress—cousin Melanie."

"Come on, let's run." Todd was blushing as Will chuckled and got to his feet.

"Hey, hotshot," someone called out, "trying to get this rookie ready for the big show?"

Just then, two of Highfield's popular guys, juniors Rudy Swart and Gates Cooper, ran over to the field. That was Rudy with the wisecrack. Both of them were starters on the varsity. Rudy was a muscular defender, built like a tank, stocky and powerful. He had close-cropped dark hair, and his shorts hung below his knees. Gates was tall, blond, and good-looking, hair combed perfectly. He was slick, always with a smirk on his face, as if he could make fun of somebody just by looking at him.

"Greetings, bunglers," Will answered. "My man Todd's all ready to go. Better hold on to your starting spot, Gates, or you'll be riding the pine."

Gates sneered at that comment, but Todd thought there was something else in his look. Maybe he wasn't so sure of his starting spot with Todd moving up to varsity.

"Hey," Will called out, "let's go two on two."

Rudy stopped, but Gates called across the field to the girls, who were almost gone.

"Hey, Mel! Wait up!" Then to Rudy, "Come on, time's a waistin'."

They trotted off. Todd watched as they confidently joked and laughed with Melanie and her friends while they all walked away. He wished he could be that confident, especially with Melanie. But it was tough to outdo a good-looking junior like Gates when you were just a freshman.

Thump! The ball hit him on the shoulder.

"They're chumps," Will said. "Don't worry. Mel will never go for Gates. And, hey, you're on varsity now—got newfound status."

On varsity. Right. Highfield High varsity boys soccer. Wow. One of the best teams in the state. Todd took a deep breath. He saw Gates put an arm around Melanie, who shook it off.

That was good to see.

✧✧✧✧

Todd was flying high when he got home. He was eager to tell his parents that Coach Jaynes was giving him a tryout on varsity. He hurried up the walk to the kitchen door. The Benson house was like a lot of others in Highfield. It was a one-family, built in the 1950s, with a nice lawn and flower gardens.

Todd's parents were experts with flowers because his mother's family owned greenhouses down in Ross Corners, a town about twenty miles away. There, they grew flowers to sell to florists all across the country. Todd's grandparents were retiring from the business, and his parents had taken it over.

Mrs. Benson was the one who knew about plants, while Mr. Benson ran the business side of the operation. His father's real specialty was soccer—at least until he hurt his knee badly in a semipro game a few years ago. He'd taught Todd how to play, especially how to dribble and shoot. Mr. Benson was excited to hear the news.

"Well, son, just don't let it go to your head," Mr. Benson said, as they made their way to the dinner table. "And remember, some of those guys are much bigger than you, so you have to play smarter than them."

The talk at the table was of soccer, as it often was in the Benson house. Even his ten-year-old sister, Betsy, had advice for Todd. But it wasn't about soccer. It was something about how to impress the girls, especially Melanie. Todd didn't listen to her.

CHAPTER TWO

The Rookie

Todd and Will headed for the varsity soccer field on Monday afternoon. They both lived in town, near the high school. It was a beautiful fall day. Todd couldn't have felt better as they walked along under maple trees that shaded the sidewalk. The leaves were already turning gold and orange.

They passed the tennis courts, where the girls' team was working out. There was Melanie, hitting against the wall. She was strong, ripping the ball backhand and forehand. Her hair twisted in a tight braid flapped against her back every time she swung. She was as good an athlete as she was pretty.

"Greetings, cuz!" Will called out to his cousin, and she turned to wave.

"Congrats, Todd," she said, clenching the racket above her head. "Heard you're on varsity!"

Todd wasn't ready with an answer. He just grinned sheepishly.

"Gonna try to stay on the team."

His voice broke a bit, and he waved—forgetting he held his soccer shoes. One clunked him on the nose.

Melanie still smiled as they went past.

Will said, "The damsel gazes upon you fondly, my man."

Todd didn't answer, but he hoped Will was right. Now he started feeling nervous about his first varsity practice. Was he good enough?

Todd and Will got to the field early, before practice began. They wanted to do their regular routine: Todd shooting and Will saving just about everything.

"Yo, Cooper, let's show the rookie a few things."

That was Rudy, striding over, with Gates tagging along. Gates, the ladies man, had that stupid grin on his face, as usual.

"What you gonna show him, chump?" Will said to Gates, tossing the ball back to Todd. "How to score? He knows that already."

"Just some survival moves goalies don't have to worry about," Rudy grinned, glancing at Gates.

"Hey, rookie," Gates said to Todd, "you know how to go down to get a free kick?"

"Go down?" Todd asked, surprised. "I try to stay on my feet."

First, Gates pushed the ball ahead. Rudy took a defensive stance, and Gates started to dribble past him. Rudy stuck a foot in and got the ball. It was clean, but Gates went down, as if he had been tripped.

"Ref! Ref!" Gates laughed from where he lay on the ground. He raised one hand to an imaginary referee. "Foul! Red card!"

"Pretty slick," Will said, as Rudy and Gates laughed. "You dudes are slick cheaters."

"Whoa, man," Gates objected. "It's survival. They do it, so we gotta do it."

"Yeah," Rudy added angrily. "Remember the Brazil game, when they got that free kick 'cause a guy took a dive?"

Todd remembered a U.S. men's national team game against Brazil in an important tournament. A Brazilian player went down just the same way. At first, it looked like he'd been tripped. But the replay showed he had actually tripped himself on purpose.

"Show the rookie again, Cooper," Rudy said, stepping back as Gates got up.

Gates then showed how he did it. As he dribbled, he brought his back foot forward to hit the heel of his front foot. If a defender was close, it would look like a foul.

Will said, "It's cheating."

"Call it what you want," Rudy said. "But that free kick resulted in a goal against the U.S."

"How do you learn that stuff?" Todd asked.

"Practice," Will answered for them. "They watch the pro games on TV and study the flopper replays."

Gates booted the ball away and turned to Todd.

"Rookie, you want to be on varsity, you best get with the program," Gates said. "Coach Jaynes wants us to know how to survive against the enemy."

"Yeah, it's a hard world out there," Will grumbled and scoffed.

"You got game, man?" Rudy said to Todd. "If not, you don't belong on the Highfield varsity."

"Maybe I do, or—" Todd glanced at Will, who stretched his legs and turned away from them.

"Coach Jaynes," Gates said, "don't take maybe for an answer."

Todd knew what he meant. Highfield High was the best. It was expected to challenge for the state championship again this year. Jaynes had won it three times in the past ten years.

By now, most of the team was on the field, warming up or kicking balls around.

"Coach wants only great results on the field," Rudy said.

"You got that right!" Will cut in. "That's why Benson's on the squad. Coach wants somebody who can score goals."

Gates flushed at that comment. Gates was the Highfield starting striker. He was supposed to score. He was the star, the pretty-boy junior all the girls admired. Maybe even Melanie.

"Come on, man," Rudy said to Todd. "Give it a try."

"I don't dive," Todd said, sorry he had to have trouble with these guys before the first practice. "I obey the rules—"

"Obey!" Gates laughed. "Okay, so you're Mr. Obedient! Obeey Obedient."

Todd could have said it was cheating to fake a foul. The ref could give a player a warning— a yellow card—if the player dived. Two warnings would earn a red card, and the player would be kicked out of the game. But Todd didn't say anything. They knew the rules well enough.

"Okay, Obeey," Rudy kicked a ball to Todd and set up like a defender. "Show me what you got."

"Leave him in the dust, Todd," Will said.

"Get by me, Obeey." Rudy crouched low, ready to stop Todd's dribble.

Rudy was big, wide, and strong. His muscular legs looked like tree trunks, and his broad shoulders filled out his T-shirt. Todd took a breath and then pulled the ball back to get some dribbling room.

"Give him a lesson," Gates said.

Todd left the ball between them, tempting Rudy.

Will said, "Go get it from him, chump."

As Todd expected, Rudy stepped forward, big steps—right foot first, left foot, right foot . . .

Todd faked toward Rudy's left. Rudy's left foot came out. Todd faked again, this time to Rudy's right. Rudy thought this was the move. Now all his weight was on his left foot as he threw his right foot out to block the ball.

Instead, the ball was already past him, skipping over his left foot, which was planted and couldn't move. In the same instant, Todd neatly jumped over that foot and past him.

Will hooted. Rudy was frustrated and turned for another challenge. Todd faked him out again, and Rudy was caught flat-footed. The third time, Todd nutmegged him—played the ball between his legs, making Rudy look helpless. Just then, the coach blew the whistle for the start of practice. Todd realized the whole team and the coach had

seen him beat Rudy. And Rudy was the varsity's best defender.

"Try and get away with that in the scrimmage, Obeey," Gates said, glancing at Rudy, who looked annoyed.

Jaynes called them all in. Todd's first varsity practice was starting. Could he keep up?

CHAPTER THREE

Ready for Varsity?

"Okay, team," Coach Jaynes called out as the varsity players trotted over and sat down in front of him. "Benson here's gonna get his chance, and we'll see if he's good enough."

"Hey, Obeey," Rudy called over. "Ain't jayvee no more."

Todd looked at Jaynes, with his black mustache and heavy eyebrows. Short and thickset, he wore a baseball hat and a jet-black training suit with white stripes up the side. The coach grinned at Rudy's comment.

"That's right, Benson." He didn't bother to look at Todd. "Got to up your game here. Now, five laps with sprints! Rudy, take them around."

The players jumped to their feet and formed two single-file lines behind Rudy and Gates. They ran around the field at a good pace. Will was next to Todd, near the end of the lines.

"So that's it?" Todd asked him quietly.

"Forsooth, dude," Will said. He knew what Todd meant. "That's all the welcome you'll get from Coach. Least till you prove yourself."

Rudy yelled "Go!" and Will and Todd sprinted to the front of the line. Every time Rudy shouted, the two players at the end sprinted to the front. Most of them said a good word to Todd as they ran past him. At least most of the team welcomed him.

After warm-ups and some heading drills, Jaynes organized several four-on-four games. The goalies worked out together, while the field players played with cones for goals. Todd found himself playing against Gates and Rudy. He didn't know how his own three teammates usually played, so it took a while to learn each other's moves. There was a lot of one-touch passing. Everybody hustled and played hard, as Coach Jaynes demanded.

"What you do in practice, you do in the game," Jaynes called out from time to time. "Move the ball, move it quick."

Jaynes often yelled at guys for holding the ball too long. He didn't much care for dribbling. And dribbling was what Todd did best.

"Get rid of it, Benson!" Jaynes would yell. "Pass it and get open!"

It didn't surprise Todd that Rudy and Gates took him down a few times. He tried to ignore it, but his legs were bruised and scraped from their tackles. Often, he beat them, and he scored a few times. His team was ahead when Jaynes called out, "Next goal wins!"

Will was watching now, and he called out, "Nutmeg 'em, rookie!"

But now Gates had the ball and took off up the middle, straight for the cones. That caught Todd's teammates by surprise. But not him. He got there just in time to block what Gates thought would be an easy goal. In the next moment, Todd was breaking away. He realized that varsity players were not so hard to beat after all.

Then he was flat on his face, tripped from behind. As he rolled, he saw Gates getting the loose ball. Todd was dazed. He'd gone down hard. He tried to sit up to clear his head.

There was Will, grabbing Gates by the shirtfront and heaving him back. Rudy came in and pushed at Will, but Jaynes shouted at them.

"It's over! Break it up. Take it easy, guys. Don't want injuries."

Jaynes glanced at Todd, who was on his feet by now, refusing to show he had been shaken up. His ears were ringing. Will asked if he was all right. Todd clenched his jaw and nodded.

The coach's whistle blasted, and he called everyone in. He said there was an away game the next day. It would be an easy game against Ross Corners, the league's weakest team. He told them he wanted a lot of goals.

"Looks like Benson can take a hit," Jaynes smirked, still not looking at Todd. "Tomorrow he'll get a chance to show us if he's ready for varsity."

Todd wanted to rub his sore muscles, but he refused to show any sign of pain. At least the ringing in his ears had stopped. Not until he and Will were walking home did he admit he ached.

"The Ross Corners game is your debut, dude." Will slapped him on the shoulder. "Start scoring, and Gates'll be riding the pine."

"Yeah," Todd said, knowing his trouble with Gates and Rudy had just begun.

The Ross Corners match was special to Todd not just because it was his first varsity game. It seemed his whole family was involved somehow. Both his parents came to the game, and Betsy, too, of course. Two of the players on the other team were Todd's cousins, and their families were there as well. He worked with them all at the Ross Corners greenhouse during the summer. Even a few employees from the business came over to watch the game.

Then there was Melanie, who'd driven down with her older tennis teammates. Mel's being there made Todd more nervous than anything. Her tennis match had been canceled because it was a rainy day. Heavy rain that morning had turned into a soft drizzle. The fans wore rain jackets and held umbrellas. But it was a mild day, and Todd enjoyed the excitement of it all. Will was not so pleased.

The Ross Corners field was sloppy and slippery. A big puddle of water covered one penalty area.

Will saw it and said "odds bodkins." He pushed at the water with a foot, but there was too much to clear it away. "Shoulda brought my wet suit and scuba gear."

Todd knew a slippery field gave the advantage to the attacker. The attacker should know where he wanted to go with the ball, while the defender had to react. It wasn't easy for the goalie to react on a sloppy field, when his feet skidded.

Warm-ups ended, and Todd hoped he'd get in for at least a quarter of the game.

"You'll play, Obeey," said Gates, as he pulled off his rain jacket.

He still looked perfect in his all-white away uniform, while everybody else was soggy and splashed with mud. "We'll run up the score and coach will let you have the crumbs."

While Highfield was undefeated, Ross Corners had not won very often this year. Highfield beat them, 4–0, the first time they had played this season. Will told Todd he heard they were getting better, though. No team had scored more than two goals against them since then.

"This year they have a new coach who's been working on their defense," Will said, about to take the field. "And their goalie is supposed to be decent."

Will didn't know how right he was.

The Ross Corners players, wearing red shirts and black shorts and socks, were sure hard to score on. In fact, through most of the first half, the score remained tied, 0–0. Highfield had several great chances to score, but the ball just wouldn't go in the goal.

No matter what Highfield did, Ross Corners players seemed to be there at the last moment. They blocked shots, made desperate tackles, or the goalie would make great acrobatic saves.

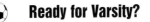

Even the wet field seemed to favor Ross Corners. Highfield controlled the game with their short passing—but they couldn't score.

Todd watched from the end of the bench. The Highfield players were getting frustrated, which made them play worse. Ross Corners was supposed to be weak. But they kept most of their players on defense. They "packed it in," as was the saying. Highfield played very rough, but Ross Corners was able to take it.

As the half drew to a close, Coach Jaynes's face turned redder and redder. He liked to sit on a director's chair and look cool. But today, he was steamed. Every time Highfield missed a chance or lost the ball, he gulped down water from a plastic bottle he kept under his seat. He began to yell whenever a player lost the ball on the dribble.

"Piddling with the ball," he called it.

The crowd was thrilled—especially the Ross Corners gang. They were yelling and clapping every time their players touched the ball or made a good defensive play. But every time a Highfield player did something wrong, their fans groaned. Coach Jaynes gulped. That water bottle was almost empty.

Gates was hopeless out there. It was as if he didn't want to get any mud on his uniform. The mud was exhausting to run in, and the poor guy always seemed to get the ball in that standing water. One time, the Ross Corners goalie dived in for the ball and splashed water all over Gates. He stood back and thoroughly wiped his face with his shirt before continuing to play.

That got a few gulps from Coach Jaynes. He threw the empty water bottle. Even Rudy yelled at Gates. Then, in the last minutes of the half, Ross Corners broke away. Will came out, but Rudy got there first. Rudy lunged in and knocked the ball away. But to his horror, the ball squirted past Will and into the goal.

"Gadzooks!" Will exploded in dismay.

Rudy lay there, head in hands. Ross Corners fans went delirious. Will yanked Rudy to his feet and put an arm over his shoulder. He didn't want Rudy to feel bad. It was a mistake, but it came from a great effort.

The whistle soon blew for halftime, and the Ross Corners fans exploded again, cheering wildly. The players sloshed off the field.

The score was Ross Corners 1, Highfield 0. Todd's teammates and Coach Jaynes couldn't believe it.

CHAPTER FOUR

The Enemy

As Todd went to sit with the team for the coach's halftime talk, he looked over at his father. Mr. Benson was trying not to grin. Todd knew he didn't much like Coach Jaynes, although he'd been careful not to say so directly.

The coach's halftime speech shocked Todd. He'd never seen a man in his mid-fifties get so angry before. Coach Jaynes wasn't screaming, but he was boiling over. His icy stare locked onto his players—especially Gates, who had played so miserably in the first half. He spoke through clenched teeth, and sometimes spit came out.

"We're gonna mop the floor with them next half! I know that! But if you play like this against good teams, then you can forget about the state championship. You get it?"

Some of the players tried to agree with him, but they all seemed in shock at being behind to a so-called lousy team. Rudy sat there, looking glum—elbows on his knees, head down.

Jaynes said a few things about how weak the opposition was and about how they got a goal by a "stupid mistake." That wasn't true, because Rudy had made a great defensive play. It was just bad luck the ball went in.

"Hey, Coach, what do you mean?" To everyone's surprise, Will had spoken up. "Rudy's been the best player out there today, Coach, he—"

"Awright, awright, whatever, let's get back to business." Jaynes didn't like to be challenged, but Will could stand up to him because he was so important to the team. "Benson, you're in on the left side. . . ."

Todd wondered if he'd heard that correctly. Already?

"Your job's to chase the ball and cross it. Don't dribble. Don't piddle with it. Use your speed. Then get it over to Gates. Set him up. And Cooper, finish it!" Coach said.

The plan was for the defenders in the back and Will to boot everything long to Todd. He was fresh, and he was fast. But as he went onto the field, his legs felt like jelly. At the last minute, Jaynes called him over.

"I know you have family on the other team, Benson, but when you're on the field, they're not family, they're not friends—listen up." He drew Todd closer. "Today, on the field, they're the enemy. And you better play like they're the enemy. All right, go!"

They're the enemy.

Those words echoed in Todd's mind as he took his position as a left-side attacker. He would be on the same side as the Highfield fans. His family and Mel were there. At first, all he could think of was what Coach Jaynes had said. His own cousins were supposed to be the enemy?

The game restarted. Before long, Todd loosened up. He shook off the awful words of his coach.

He wanted the ball. He concentrated on the game. Not on the coach. Not the fans, not family, not the mud or the rain. He was in a varsity game! And he knew he could do it.

At least on the ground. A big Ross Corners defender got to the high balls most of the time. Their team had been well coached on defensive heading. But on the ground, Todd used his speed and took advantage of the defenders' bad footing in the mud. He began to create chance after chance for Highfield. Unfortunately, it was Gates at the other end of those chances, and today he was hopeless.

In one situation, Highfield had a free kick that Rudy sent sailing into the Ross Corners goalmouth. Todd went up for it. It was a great chance for a goal. But that big, strong defender came out of nowhere and headed the ball clear, almost off Todd's own head.

"Get your elbows up next time, Obeey!" Rudy said, as they ran back on defense. "Get 'em up and use 'em to keep that guy off you."

Todd knew playing like that could be dangerous to the opposing player. He also knew time was running out. Ross Corners packed it in even more. It seemed like every guy they had was on defense. Another Highfield free kick, and Rudy got ready to take it. He told Gates to go to the right of the goal where he'd take defenders with him. Then he spoke quietly to Todd.

"Start right, then go to the far post, Obeey. You're getting it. And keep your elbows up. I ain't losing this game on an own-goal, man!"

What followed was a blur, it happened so fast. Todd sprinted right. He heard the whistle for the kick and cut back across the goalmouth. He turned. The ball was there in the air. He jumped. He had it. And his elbows were up. He directed the ball downward, and it squirted on the mud and into the corner of the goal. 1–1!

The Highfield fans went wild. Everybody on the team grabbed him, high-fiving, and slapping his back. Even Coach Jaynes was on his feet, beaming. Then Todd saw his father, looking back at something on the field. So was Melanie. The ref blew his whistle over and over. Todd turned to see the big defender lying on the goal line, holding his forehead, blood on his hands.

Todd had elbowed him. It was an accident, but it was awful just the same. Some Ross Corners fans were shouting for a red card. Todd stood there, staring in disbelief. The ref waved off the call for a foul. Somebody on the sidelines said the refs always favored Highfield and that gave them an advantage.

"Let's go, Obeey!" Rudy pulled Todd toward their own half for the restart. "We need another one. Fifteen minutes left!"

As he went, Todd looked at his father, who seemed pained. Todd held his hands out to say it was an accident. His father nodded.

"Great play, Benson!" That was Coach Jaynes yelling. "Now keep playing! Remember what I told you!"

This was the enemy?

Todd felt terrible. His legs went weak again. The defender was on the sidelines now, sitting up. His coach treated his forehead. The refs were there, too, making sure the player was all right. Both teams were taking the break to drink water. Will tossed a bottle to Todd.

"Not intentional, man." As he turned away to his goal, Will said quietly, "But next time, be careful with your elbows."

Play began again. At first, Todd was in a daze. He didn't know how to react to the play he'd just made. But he knew he had to keep playing.

Then, to his surprise, the defender that he had knocked down came running back onto the field. A butterfly bandage was over one eyebrow. Todd offered his hand.

"Hey, man, sorry . . . "

"Yeah," said the boy, lightly slapping Todd's hand. "You Highfield guys always apologize for playing dirty—when you score."

"Dirty?"

"That's the only way you can win."

Todd was startled at first. He didn't deserve that rude comment. He wasn't a dirty player. Anger rose up in him. Now he had something else to prove. He turned to Rudy.

"Gimme the ball on the ground next time, in front of this guy."

Rudy didn't question Todd. And when the chance came, he played him a ball that stopped in the puddle, almost in reach of the defender. Todd charged and faked to boot the ball at goal. The defender threw himself to block it and skidded past. In the next moment, Todd was sloshing by him. The mud was terrible. The goalie was charging. The only thing Todd could do was toe the ball as hard as he could.

It zipped past the goalie's ear. Highfield 2, Ross Corners 1.

This time, the Bensons and Melanie all cheered. The Highfield fans all cheered Todd's great effort. Coach Jaynes applauded. A couple more minutes went by, and the game was over. Todd felt like a wet rag, completely spent.

Melanie passed by, tapped his arm, and said he'd played a great game. She said nothing to Gates, who looked miffed. Todd was thrilled. It could not have been a better start on the Highfield varsity.

The Bensons all bundled, wet and steaming, into the car. As they drove away, Todd was jabbering about the game, until he realized everybody else was quiet. He asked why.

"Well, Todd," Mrs. Benson said, "we have a big announcement to make."

She cleared her throat. His father cleared his throat and looked at her. They both seemed ready to speak, but paused.

Then Betsy piped up excitedly. "We're moving to Ross Corners next year!"

Leaving Highfield

When the Bensons got home that evening, Todd's very exciting day had turned to a very mixed-up day. By now, his parents had explained that Mrs. Benson's mother and father were retiring and moving to a new apartment. They were leaving the Ross Corners farmhouse and flower business with the greenhouse to the Bensons.

Todd's family agreed not to tell anyone else about the move until Thanksgiving. Todd could not even tell Will. By then, Todd's soccer season would be over. Coach Jaynes wouldn't have to wonder whether to put him back on jayvee and give some other young player a chance—one who was staying at Highfield.

On the one hand, Todd loved his grandparents' old farmhouse, with its barn, woods, and fields. On the other, he felt he was about to become an important player on one of the best high school soccer teams in the state.

Like Will, Todd had high hopes of a college soccer scholarship. But Will was a great goalie on a great team. Scouts would know about him. Todd soon would be a good player on an ordinary team. No scouts would likely hear about him. If he did not get noticed, his chances of a soccer scholarship would disappear. He told his father so.

"Why do you say that?" Mr. Benson asked.

They were sitting in the kitchen, and Todd was rubbing his bruised legs with liniment.

"Come on, Dad, just 'cause they almost beat us today doesn't mean anything. They got lucky. Could've been ten zip us. Should've."

"Coulda, shoulda, woulda—that's not much of an attitude, is it? Fact is, Ross Corners might have snatched the win."

Mr. Benson was right. But Todd was right, too. They'd outplayed Ross Corners by miles, and if just—well, shoulda, coulda, woulda. . . . Still, Todd's future in soccer seemed hopeless playing for a weak team compared to Highfield.

"No chance for a soccer scholarship, Dad." He let his pants leg down, making a face as he felt the pain of a bruised shinbone. "But their fullback was tough."

"Jerry Spane," Mrs. Benson said, passing through the room. "Good family. I went to high school with his parents."

There it was again. Talk about Ross Corners as if it already was home. Or always had been, since the Bensons had spent so much time there for as long as Todd could remember.

Betsy breezed in behind her mother. "You're just sorry to be moving because of Mel," she said.

Todd flushed. His father said he should remember they were moving only twenty miles away.

"Anyway, Ross Corners has a very good coach these days," he added.

Todd just shrugged.

Mr. Benson said, "And the coach told me they're expecting a Brazilian exchange student— a guy who plays club soccer at home."

That got Todd's attention. And something else did, too.

"You mean you know their coach?"

"Comes into the greenhouse sometimes. New in town. Was a top-notch college player. Midfielder. Took a lot of coaching courses. Plans to coach at the college level one day. His name is Jim Godwin—"

"Geez, Dad, you got it all figured out already." Todd was surprised to hear all this. "Anything else I should know?"

"Yes, he was quite impressed with you today."

Todd was startled to hear that the Ross Corners coach had said that to his father.

"You say that we're moving there?"

"Not yet, of course."

"Hope he doesn't want his players to be floppers," Todd grumbled and then remembered that elbow he'd used. "And, oh man, I hope he doesn't think I intentionally. . . . "

"No," Mr. Benson chuckled. "He saw the whole play. Even if your elbows were not where they should've been."

Todd could overhear Betsy's voice from the other room. "It's a secret, Amanda. I can't say! No, not even to you."

She was on the phone with Amanda Weatherly, Melanie's younger sister. They were best friends. As Betsy kept saying she had to keep a secret, Todd sighed.

"No way she'll keep it quiet about us moving, Dad. Mel will be the first one in high school to know about it."

Mr. Benson said they should wait and see.

"Meanwhile, you play well enough so they have to keep you on varsity this season, even if next year you'll be with another team."

"The enemy," Todd mumbled.

"What's that?"

"I'll become the enemy. That's how they'll think of me here. Coach Jaynes told me during the game to think of Ross Corners as the enemy. I'll be Highfield's number-one enemy."

For once, Mr. Benson didn't have a ready reply. Just then, Todd heard Betsy say, "You have a secret, too? What? Tell me. He did? Gates? Gates asked Melanie to the junior-senior prom?"

Todd felt cold hearing that. What could he do? Gates was a cool-guy junior. Todd was just a freshman. Freshmen and sophomores didn't even go to the prom unless they were invited as a date. Todd tried to listen to the rest of Betsy's conversation, but his father cleared his throat loudly and stood up.

Instead of giving more advice, Mr. Benson took a deep breath and patted his son's leg in encouragement.

Todd winced a bit as his father touched a tender bruise. He tried not to show the pain, though, just the way he'd try not to show the pain of leaving Highfield. Or of Mel going to the prom with Gates.

A couple of weeks went by, and nobody else seemed to know about Todd and his family moving to Ross Corners—not even Will or Melanie.

As Mr. Benson advised, Todd concentrated on soccer. He played his hardest in games, worked his hardest at practice, and made himself an important starter.

Todd tried not to think about leaving Highfield. It was exciting to be on a winning team. Todd scored goals, but most of the Highfield wins came because Will was such a great goalie. He and Todd still worked out together in their spare time. They enjoyed pushing each other to get better.

Will was losing weight, and he could jump higher. Working out with Will made Todd better, too—especially placing that high ball in the far corner. Otherwise, the ball hardly ever got past Will. It seemed to stick to his hands. He always was in the right place to make even the toughest saves look easy.

Rudy and Gates still called Todd "Obeey," because he refused to flop. They didn't try to rough him up at practice anymore because he was learning how to deal with it. Todd gave as well as he took. He felt more confident and even stronger. Plus, he became the team's leading scorer, with

eight goals in six games. Gates had only five for the whole season. And he was jealous.

Gates still tried to charm Melanie. Because Rudy lived next door to her and was a childhood friend, Gates spent a lot of time there, too. Especially when Melanie was home. Todd learned this from Betsy, of course.

CHAPTER SIX

Melanie

As it turned out, Melanie actually learned the Benson secret from somebody else. And it wasn't Betsy spilling the secret to Amanda. Even Betsy had managed to keep quiet about it. Melanie found out in a way that Todd never imagined she would.

It happened one afternoon, late in October, when the weather was sunny and cold. Tennis season was almost over, but the Highfield girls were in the state tournament. They practiced every day, even when the weather was cold.

As he often did, Todd passed by the courts just to say hello to Melanie. He didn't care that she was going to the prom with Gates. Todd still thought she was one of the nicest people in Highfield. She always had a smile and a friendly word for him.

Todd felt bad to be keeping his secret from her. Well, she'd know soon enough. Soccer was almost over—a couple weeks of state tournament games to go. Then everybody would find out.

Melanie practiced her stroke by hitting tennis balls against the wall. As usual, he found a way to start a brief conversation with her. Generally, it was about Amanda—or what Betsy last told him about Amanda. Melanie would usually say something about what Amanda had told her about Betsy. It was a casual conversation, but they both seemed to enjoy it.

"Hey, Mel. Amanda still trying to give your cat a bath?" Todd asked, as he walked over to greet her.

"She actually did it yesterday! Got a few scratches, but she's determined. I hear Betsy has a plan to one-up her."

"How so?"

"Wants to give her brother a bath!"

"Right."

"Water balloons." She whacked a serve.

"I'll be ready for her. She can't keep anything secret."

"Not from me, she can't," Melanie said, "especially about you."

Todd didn't care for the sound of that.

"Like what," he asked. "What secret?"

"Oh, about all the girls you like." She hit another.

"Girls? I don't like a lot of girls. Hey, I'm just a freshman."

"So?"

"What girls are interested in a freshman? Girls are interested in . . . juniors. You should know, right?"

"Meaning?" She was holding the ball out for a serve but stopped before tossing it. "Well?"

Todd knew he'd gone too far, but there was no stopping now.

"Well, like, you're going to the prom with a junior, with Gates."

"What?" Melanie tossed the ball, took a whack at it, and rattled it off the frame. "Who told you that? Betsy?"

"Hey, sorry I mentioned it. I have to get to practice, Mel. Forget it."

But she was already busting through the gate confronting him, hands on hips. Boy was she pretty. Todd thought he would melt.

"Just joking, Mel."

"Well, Mr. Joker, I'm not going to the prom with Gates. I want to go with . . . with the person I want to go with . . . even if he's a freshman."

That was when Todd realized she meant him. He swallowed hard and tried to talk but was tongue-tied.

Melanie had the most beautiful smile he'd ever seen. She was saying she'd wait until he was a junior, and then go with—

"Oh, no." He remembered what she didn't know yet.

"What?" She stepped back. "Why say oh, no? Don't you? . . . "

"Yes . . . I mean, no, I mean I won't . . . I won't be here—at Highfield then, or even before then."

That was when he told Melanie everything. Behind his words were his feelings for her. And that's how she learned that Todd was moving away. Tears came to her eyes.

"Yo, Mel, what's up?" Gates and Rudy appeared, swaggering along the path.

Melanie turned away, back to the tennis, and started serving, harder than ever. None of her serves went in, though. In fact, not one even got over the net.

"Hey, Obeey, what'd you just say to her?" Rudy asked.

Todd swung to face him and growled, "Call me that again and I'll kick your butt, Rudy!"

Rudy was startled but not worried. It was Gates who cackled.

"You gonna let him talk like that to you, man?"

Rudy was confused at first, and then anger started coming.

Gates said, "I can't believe you're gonna let this—"

"Stop it!" Melanie shrieked.

"Yeah, stop it." That was Will. "Back off, unless you want to call Todd names yourself, Gates."

Todd was ready for Gates to dare insult him. There was a long, tense silence. Gates turned pale, his mouth working. But Rudy and Will weren't backing off.

Melanie saved the day. "Please, I'm asking you all to stop! Please!"

Gates bobbed his head. "Okay, Mel, for you."

Gates and Rudy left, and Todd's heart pounded with anger. Melanie was anxious, eyes wide. Will, though, was calm as ever, and grinning.

"Off we go to practice, Pelé. Then you can kick their butts on the field." He winked at Melanie. "How could you ever go to prom with that dufus?"

"What? I am not!" Mel protested. "How did you know he asked me?"

Will laughed.

"Gates told me he was going to get you to go with him. Bet me five bucks. Now I know you refused, and I can collect from him."

Todd tried not to laugh. So did Melanie. But they both did.

Then they became serious again. They were thinking about Todd moving away. Will, still chuckling, noticed something was wrong.

"Hey, what's up with you guys? You seem . . ."

Will shut up when he saw Melanie had tears in her eyes. She went back to the tennis as Todd told his friend the news.

"Doom and gloom!" Will gasped. "Highfalutin' Highfield to rustic Ross Corners?" He tried to grin and be easygoing, as usual. "But you're just getting warmed up here, bro, you're just getting started—"

"I know." Todd glanced at Melanie unhappily whacking the ball against the wall, over and over. "Believe me, I know."

CHAPTER SEVEN

The Rockets

The Highfield boys varsity soccer season didn't end the way Coach Jaynes had planned it. They didn't win the state championship. But it was even worse than that. Will injured his left ankle in one of the early state tournament games. When Will had to leave the game, Highfield became just a good team, not a great one. They scored twice, but the other team scored three times.

Will was miserable. His lower left leg was put in a Velcro-wrapped brace to protect the muscles and ligaments.

Although he could walk on it after a week or so, Will could hardly joke about his injury or toss out one of his wacky phrases. Except once in a while, Todd heard him grumble under his breath, "Ye gods, it stings."

Todd wasn't sure whether Will meant his injury hurt so much or that it might shoot down his hopes for a college soccer scholarship. Probably both, said Melanie, who worried about her cousin being so unhappy.

A couple weeks after the injury, Melanie sent Todd an instant message. "W's crushed more than anybody on the team."

"I know," Todd replied. "Next year's W's last chance."

"2 bad u won't b on the team."

"No, I'll b buried in rustic R.C. Invisible."

"U'll do well."

"Thnxs. And I'll be the N-M-EE."

"LoL. Not to Will. Or me."

"Not u! Good. Will, tho."

Melanie didn't reply to that. She said Rudy had just dropped in.

"Wants to watch a Man U. game on my laptop."

"Gates, too?"

"Naturally. Gotta go. Amanda's washing the cat again."

Todd knew Melanie's father was a longtime friend of Rudy's father. Rudy had been a friend of Melanie's since childhood. He often watched sports on the Weatherly television or Mel's new laptop. Too bad Gates showed up with him.

So, the Highfield boys' soccer season ended with a dull thud. Or, as Will put it when he started to feel better, "Not with a bang, but a whimper." Some poetry reference. As for Todd, he'd been high scorer, with thirteen goals. But Coach Jaynes never thanked him or wished him good luck.

"At least he didn't call me the enemy yet," Todd told Will. "But I guess I always will be to Rudy and Gates."

"Forsooth, you will be, sport."

A few weeks later, on a Saturday afternoon in December, Todd and Will took the Benson pickup loaded with moving boxes to the farmhouse at Ross Corners. The Bensons had already begun moving some of their belongings. Will could drive, because his right leg was fine.

"Hey, Benson, about next season." He looked over at Todd and gave a confident smile. "I'll be covering that far corner whenever you show up in front of my goal."

Todd had to chuckle. Then it hit him hard to think he'd have to score against Will when they met on the field. Todd felt bad thinking about scoring on his friend. It was only fun scoring on him when they practiced together.

Todd said, "Strange to think about playing *against* you, man."

"Don't worry, Pelé," Will teased. "By fall, I'll be fifteen pounds lighter, and you won't float anything over my head."

"Ross Corners only plays defense, not much offense," Todd said. "Fat chance I'll have to make you look. . . . "

"Good?" Will countered. "Make me look good saving your best stuff?"

Todd was going to say "bad" and normally would have tossed out that sort of wisecrack. But he held back. Making Will look bad was the last thing he wanted to do.

He looked out the window, trying not to think of what would happen if and when he had to score on Will in a game. He wanted Will to win the state tournament, to get that scholarship. . . .

"Well, Pelé? Make me look good?"

"Lucky," Todd replied. "Make you look lucky, what else?"

"Forsooth, sport." Will laughed in that hearty way of his. "Goalies need luck, like Napoleon said—or was that about generals?"

Todd hadn't heard Will laugh like that for weeks. He was glad to see his friend recovering from the injury and the disappointment.

✧✧✧✧

Winter passed, and spring arrived. So did the club soccer season. The Bensons planned to move to Ross Corners by mid-summer. That meant Todd could play one more season with the Rockets, Highfield's under-nineteen traveling team. He'd heard in a text message from Melanie that Coach Jaynes had told the traveling team's coach not to let Todd play.

Only Highfield players should be allowed on the Rockets, Jaynes had said. The Rockets coach ignored Jaynes.

"Ur 2 good," Melanie wrote. "Rockets coach wants u even if u r Coach J's N-M-EE."

Though he was the youngest player in the entire U-19 league, Todd's ability to score goals made him a starter with the Rockets. The team had mostly Highfield juniors and seniors (including Gates and Rudy) and a few college freshmen. Although the club league was tougher than high school, the Rockets still won all their games.

They played their last game of the season on a steamy summer's day. It was a home game against the newly formed traveling team from Ross Corners. The Rockets wore purple, Ross Corners red and black.

Playing up front, Todd hardly got the ball because Gates and Rudy seldom passed it to him. When he did get it, he almost dribbled through the entire defense. But three times he was stopped by that big defender, Jerry Spane. Gates and Rudy were upset.

"Pass the ball!" Gates yelled after Todd lost it for the third time.

"Stop piddling with it!" somebody shouted.

That was Coach Jaynes, standing under a tree.

"Yeah!" Rudy chimed in. "Stop piddling with the ball!"

He and Gates were getting frustrated that they couldn't score. They took their anger out on Todd. He was steaming at all their comments. Still, he kept his emotions under control. He figured the best way to shut them all up was to score.

But it wasn't easy. The defense was tough, and there was one new guy on the Ross Corners team, Giorgio. He was short and fast, with muscular legs. He seemed to cover the whole field with ease. He almost scored twice.

At halftime, Mr. Benson came over to where Todd was sitting. Sloshing water over his face, he attempted to cool down. But the heat was intense. Todd was exhausted, though there was another half to go.

"Makes you tired when they stop your dribble." Mr. Benson knew, since he'd been a striker in his college days. "But you'll crack them next half."

"Next half? That Giorgio guy's got the ball all the time. Man, can he dribble."

"He is Brazilian," Mr. Benson said. "He's the exchange student. He'll be on your new team come fall."

"Odds bodkins!"

That was Will, sitting nearby. His leg was almost fully healed, but he couldn't play games yet. He was doing a lot of running and weight training. For sure, he'd be lighter and stronger next season.

Someone spoke to Todd from behind. "Mind if I make a suggestion, young man?"

This was a familiar face, a handsome fellow in his thirties, in a T-shirt and shorts. He'd been standing with Mr. Benson all game. Now he leaned over to Todd.

"Make the ball do the work, Todd. Don't dribble into the defense. But when you see an opening, push it past the defenders—right between them."

"Then use your speed," Mr. Benson added.

"Pretend you're going to dribble and pull them toward you," said the other man. "Then, when they come, push it and take off."

The whistle blew for the second half to begin. The other man moved away, and Todd asked his father who he was.

"That's Jim Godwin, your coach next year."

Todd was surprised. Coach Godwin looked like a soccer player, like he could step on the field right now.

And the tactic worked. Twice he held the ball and drew Jerry and another defender toward him. He ignored the shouts to pass. Then he shoved the ball between them and broke away. He scored both times.

Todd's coach kept two guys covering Giorgio most of the time. He hardly got the ball in the second half. As the end of the game approached, Todd's team was up, 2–0.

Then, for no good reason, Gates and Rudy sandwiched Jerry. They were all going for a high ball in front of the goalmouth when Rudy hit him high and Gates went in low. Rudy's challenge was clean, but Gates intended to foul. Jerry came down hard on his back, with a grunt. The ref missed the foul, but Todd shouted in anger, yanking both of them by the shirt at the same time.

"You chumps!"

Rudy and Gates grabbed him in return, and Todd swung at them. Other players jumped in to stop the fight. Jerry was there, so he was not hurt. The ref stepped in, his whistle blasting.

The scuffle ended as quickly as it started. On the sidelines, Coach Jaynes was grinning for some reason. Todd's chest heaved for air. Gates, however, had a bloody lip. Todd felt a scrape on his knuckles and realized he'd caught Gates with a punch.

The game was over now, and the ref told them all to calm down. The ref could have given red cards, but the season was over. A red card would have meant suspension for at least a game. Todd was lucky.

When Todd came off the field, his father introduced him to Mr. Godwin, the Ross Corners coach.

"Thanks for sticking up for Jerry," Mr. Godwin said as they shook hands. "And I like the way you hold the ball, not afraid to dribble."

Before everyone went home, Todd met all the Ross Corners players. They were friendly guys, all of them glad he was coming to their school. Todd met Jerry last, and he touched his forehead, just above the eyebrow. A small white scar was there.

"My doing?" Todd asked, feeling guilty.

"Yeah," Jerry grinned and offered his hand. "But now we're even."

For the first time, Todd thought being invisible in Ross Corners might not be so bad after all.

CHAPTER EIGHT

"The Ball Is Your Friend"

Todd and Will worked out together one last time before their high school seasons started. It was at the Highfield soccer field on a morning early in September. Todd's mother had driven him up while she was doing errands in town. Official practice had begun, and both knew how good their own teams would be. They took a water break and sat down to catch up on things.

Will didn't have to say much, of course, because Todd knew the Highfield players and coach. For his part, Todd was even more enthusiastic about Ross Corners than he'd been when he first came to the Highfield varsity.

"Coach Godwin has us organized great on defense, and Jerry is terrific—"

"And the goalie?"

"Not as lucky as you, but good," Todd joked.

"Any decent strikers?"

"Pretty good, but the key guy is our center midfielder, Giorgio. Great player, all the Brazilian technique and speed—"

"And floppery?"

"Huh?"

"Diver par excellence?"

"No, actually. He doesn't play that way. He told me a lot of pro players on the big teams play like that in Brazil, but amateur teams play hard—just like Pelé did."

Todd and Will had seen footage of the great Brazilian star of the twentieth century. Pelé never dove. Instead, he fought to stay on his feet. He usually drew fierce tackles and fouls.

Todd said, "Giorgio adores Pelé."

"Like you do, dude?"

"Man, I'd be happy just to play like Giorgio."

"So, you see much of cousin Mel these days?" Will asked.

That was the only problem. Those twenty miles between them were a long way when neither had a car yet.

"Just a few phone calls and text messages, but e-mails mostly," Todd said. "She was away at tennis camp for almost a month."

"And she's always got those two chumps crowding her, which is to be expected, Rudy living next door and all," Will said.

"Betsy keeps me updated on all that. She and Amanda are always gabbing on the phone or texting nonstop."

"Ye gods! But Rudy and Gates are chumps. Too bad they didn't move away instead of you, dude."

Todd didn't say it, but he actually liked playing for Ross Corners better than for Highfield. A lot better. For one thing, Coach Godwin was super, and he liked players to control the ball and try to do something with it—what Jaynes called "piddling with the ball."

They went back out on the field. Todd fired more shots at Will, who saved almost all of them.

"Hey, Pelé, give me that lob into the corner."

They practiced again and again, with Todd approaching from thirty yards on one side or the other of the goal. Will would seem to come out and commit, and Todd would loft the ball. But Will got to it every time. It was like he knew where it was going even before Todd kicked it.

"Man, you're luckier than ever!" Todd said at last.

Will just laughed. "Hey, it's not a game situation, so no pressure."

Afterward, Todd wondered how Will had stopped every one of those high floaters. He really was better than ever. This was his year. He had to get that scholarship. Todd didn't want to do anything to stand in his way. He still couldn't imagine scoring against Will in a real game.

The soccer season started out fast and roared along. Ross Corners surprised everybody as they won game after game. Todd and Giorgio competed for high scorer, and Jerry was the anchor of the defense.

Coach Godwin seemed to know everything. He was a great teacher and a terrific soccer player. The players trusted him. For the first time in the school's history, they had six wins and no losses—tied with Highfield for first place in the conference.

Todd made some good friends at Ross Corners, including Jerry and Giorgio. Giorgio was the best player Todd had ever played with.

One thing Giorgio never did was dive. His playing truly did remind Todd of those old Pelé game films. It took a lot to knock Giorgio down. He never stayed down but bounced up right away.

Giorgio was an inch-perfect passer and super midfield player. Also, he taught Todd more dribbling techniques. He also said something Todd would always remember.

During one game, Todd seemed unable to do anything right. Ross Corners was outplaying the other team but couldn't score. Giorgio kept giving Todd great pass after great pass. But Todd missed the goal, again and again. He always shot high, over the crossbar.

By the end of the half, with the score 0–0, he'd lost confidence. By then, he was passing the ball off rather than shooting for the goal.

As they gathered for Coach Godwin's halftime talk, Todd slumped down, glumly drinking from a water bottle. When Giorgio sat next to him, Todd shook his head.

"Sorry, man, I can't do anything today."

"You're rushing it," Giorgio said quietly, rubbing sweat from his face with a towel.

"I don't know what I'm doing." Todd looked down at the ground.

"Just hold the ball," Giorgio said. "Remember, the ball is your friend."

Todd looked at him, wondering what he meant.

"The ball is your friend, and it wants to play with you." Giorgio grinned. "So don't just pass it away. It's your friend. It wants to play."

Coach Godwin overheard Giorgio and smiled.

Todd was about to walk on the field for the second half with those words in his head: *The ball is your friend.* At the last moment, Coach Godwin called him back.

"The goals will come, Todd," he said, patting Todd's shoulder. "But remember, you have to keep the ball if you want to score."

It was as if a light went on in Todd's head. His coach had shown confidence in him, even though all those first-half shots had been wasted. *The goals will come. Keep the ball.*

The chance came within a few minutes of kickoff, with another perfect pass from Giorgio. Todd was about thirty yards away, uncovered, and he turned toward the goal. A defender was coming at him. Todd wound up to shoot, but he was too far out. The defender was on him now. Todd faked a shot, the defender lunged. Todd went around him and into the penalty box.

"Shoot!" the Ross Corners crowd was yelling. "Take it! Shoot!"

Two more defenders were closing in now. Todd again faked to shoot, then to dribble. In the next instant, he pushed the ball between the surprised defenders and burst through. The goalie was coming out fast, but Todd calmly fired the ball on the ground, passing the keeper's foot by inches and into the net.

"Very nice," Giorgio laughed, hugging him. "Very nice soccer playing."

That goal started an avalanche, as Ross Corners won, 7–0, with Todd scoring three and setting up the others. It was a lesson he'd never forget, thanks to Giorgio and Coach Godwin.

Coach Godwin got the very best out of all of them. The Ross Corners defense had become confident. Defensive players were even encouraged to hold the ball when they had space to run with it upfield. Coach Godwin didn't want them always to boot it away, but to take their time, to look to make a short pass, or to dribble into the clear. If they lost it, he encouraged them instead of yelling at them. Todd couldn't have been happier.

Until there came a problem with Melanie.

Because Melanie was busy with tennis season, she and Todd didn't see each other these days. Because their schedules were so busy and usually conflicted, they didn't have time to talk on the phone either. When Todd did write her an e-mail, he seldom got an answer.

The first e-mail from Melanie that troubled him said he shouldn't e-mail, text, or call her for a while. She said she had to "study." Then, before he could reply, another e-mail said he shouldn't contact her at all for a while.

She wrote, "Just don't e-mail or call until ferther notice."

"What happened to her?" he thought. "Can't even spell *further* right?"

Soccer and school, along with helping out at the greenhouse, took up all of Todd's time. He didn't even visit Highfield. He did write one more e-mail asking how Melanie's tennis season was going. He was shocked when she wrote back:

"I know you're mr. popular. I hear the girls are all crazy about you. I told you not to contact me in any way until ferther notice. I need time to think."

Todd didn't understand. But more than that, his feelings were hurt. He was sad and confused at first. But soon, he just felt angry. He didn't want to beg her to talk to him. He was also surprised that Melanie couldn't spell "further," because she was an A student. Was that some sort of joke? Was she making a joke about putting him down?

No, Todd didn't understand it at all. When it came to Melanie, the only person he could ask was Betsy. She was still close with Amanda. So, if anybody knew what was going on, it would be Betsy.

Todd took the opportunity to talk to her when he and Betsy were planting seeds at the greenhouse. It was about sixty yards long, with raised beds of black soil filling the place. Half a dozen workers were leaning over to plant hundreds of seeds in neat rows. It was a slow task, but it gave Todd and Betsy time to talk. She seemed careful when Todd first asked about Melanie.

"I don't want to gossip." She rolled her eyes.

"Oh, of course not. But what's going on? Is Gates there all the time?" Todd asked, trying not to sound too interested.

"Sort of. You know he and Rudy like to watch sports on Melanie's laptop on the front porch all the time."

"And she's always there?"

"Oh, no. They watch auto racing and extreme sports, but she mostly likes tennis, which they don't. . . ."

"So," he began, "she's not Gates's . . ."

"Girlfriend? Amanda wishes Mel was his girlfriend. Amanda thinks Gates is awesome."

Todd didn't want to hear anything else.

More brief, unfriendly e-mails and instant messages came in from Melanie—always warning Todd not to reply. It made him miserable.

His parents suggested he make new friends, including meeting other girls. He knew they were right, but he cared about Melanie. He didn't understand why she was so set against him. It looked like their budding friendship was over.

Todd told Will about the e-mails. Will often drove down on weekends to visit him at the greenhouse. Behind the greenhouse, an old bridge crossed over a stream. Todd and Will sat on a bench overlooking the stream. There, they talked about soccer and Melanie.

"Mel seems as miserable as you, dude," Will said. "She's not out partying. Just the opposite."

"What, *studying*? She should work on her spelling, then."

Todd didn't feel much sympathy for her by now. He huffed the word "ferther."

When Will asked what that was all about, Todd explained how Melanie had said not to contact her "until *ferther* notice." Will thought it was strange that Melanie would misspell anything.

"Mel spells better than I do," he said. Then, almost to himself, he said, "Forsooth, this warrants looking into, I'll wager."

CHAPTER NINE

A Best Friend in Goal

Although the trouble with Melanie stayed in Todd's mind, he had important soccer games to get ready for. The first of the two Highfield–Ross Corners games came with both teams 8–0. The game was home for Ross Corners, but the visiting Highfield crowd was almost twice as large as the home crowd.

Jerry's father made up for the shortage of home fans, though. He was an older English fellow, and he cheered louder than anybody, even before the game began.

"Up with Ross Corners! This is your game, lads! Come on, Ross Corners!"

Mr. Spane's red hair seemed to stand on end when he got excited. And at a soccer game, he was always excited.

While stretching at midfield, Todd saw Melanie standing at the side of the bleachers. His heart jumped, and he wanted to go over to her. But she looked away. Now Todd did feel like Highfield's worst enemy.

It was the same on the field. From the start, it was a fierce battle, end to end. Gates and Rudy fouled he and Giorgio a lot. Todd knew his team was a match for the Highfield players. But could they beat Will?

It was hard even to get a shot off against him. If an attacker was anywhere near the goal, Will charged out and broke up the play. He was quicker than ever. Every ball in the penalty area was his. He was like a whirlwind in goal.

Todd didn't get many shots off, but he set up Giorgio twice with low passes inside the box. The Brazilian ripped two blistering shots, but both times Will made diving saves. Todd tried high passes that got over the defenders, but Will pulled them down every time.

Todd tried not to admire Will too much. That was distracting. But Will had become an even better goalie. He would get that scholarship. But Todd knew he had to score no matter who was in goal. But the harder he tried, the more anxious he became. He'd shoot too soon or too late. Nothing but a perfect shot had a chance against Will.

Late in the game, as a substitute was coming in, Giorgio came up to Todd. They were both sweaty, dirty, and worn out.

"Hey, man, that's your best friend in their goal, right?" When Todd answered, Giorgio said, "Yeah, I can see you don't really want to score on him, right?"

Giorgio grinned in that warm way he had, but his words were sharp. Todd didn't answer, but he wanted to say that he'd been trying hard to score. Even against Will.

Giorgio said, "A real scorer doesn't even see the goalie—just the spot on the goal where he's going to shoot it."

Todd knew he was right.

The whistle blew, and the last ten minutes began.

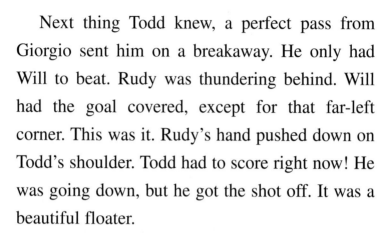

Next thing Todd knew, a perfect pass from Giorgio sent him on a breakaway. He only had Will to beat. Rudy was thundering behind. Will had the goal covered, except for that far-left corner. This was it. Rudy's hand pushed down on Todd's shoulder. Todd had to score right now! He was going down, but he got the shot off. It was a beautiful floater.

The ball was going in!

Will backpedaled, backpedaled and jumped—somehow getting his fingertips to the ball. It whacked against the post and down. Rudy booted it clear. So close. Gates and Rudy were yelling at each other for letting Todd get through. Coach Jaynes was yelling, too.

Todd yanked Will to his feet, saying, "Not next time, Lucky."

Will tugged at his goalie gloves and laughed. "Dream on, Pelé."

There wouldn't be another chance for a goal, however. In the closing minutes, Gates tripped himself inside the penalty box. Jerry made a clean tackle, but the referee didn't see it that way.

Rudy calmly scored the penalty for a 1–0 Highfield win. Gates had a very big smile on his face.

Afterward, a furious Mr. Spane complained that the referees were fooled by a fake foul. Mr. Benson interrupted and walked him away to calm him down. Will came over to shake Todd's hand. Neither one spoke about Gates's flop. Todd was too blue even to joke about "lucky" and "next time."

Then Todd saw Melanie walking past. She seemed sad and angry at the same time. He felt the same way—about her and about losing the game.

"Odds bodkins, you guys!" Will exclaimed. "Don't you even say hello to each other?"

Todd thought Melanie threw out a comment about "rude e-mails and texts." He started to say her e-mails were the rude ones. Before he could, a beaming Gates stepped in and held out a hand to Melanie.

"Hey, Mel, come ride home with me and my folks. There's a pizza party to celebrate tonight, and—"

To Todd's surprise, Melanie ignored Gates's hand. She said something about not liking "cheaters" and hurried off.

Gates turned red, kicked the ground, and stamped away.

Will said, almost to himself, "Good one, cousin Melanie."

Then he and Todd shook hands again and rejoined their teams. Todd had let his team down. If he couldn't score on Will, he was failing his new friends. No defeat had ever felt so bad. Defeat, and being the enemy.

The rest of the season went by like a blur, with Ross Corners building a 16–1 record. Todd forgot about his troubles with Melanie once he was on the soccer field. He was high scorer. No other goalie threw him off his game like Will could.

Meanwhile, Highfield was 17–0. Their rematch, home for Highfield this time, was for the league championship. A tie would give the title to Highfield.

The game was even harder fought than the first, neither team able to score. Will, as usual, was incredible. He saved everything. Todd, as usual against Highfield, played great everywhere but in front of Will's goal. As for Giorgio, he was forced to go back to help defend the goal. Highfield attacked from the wings—not trying to go up the middle, where Giorgio played. When he did get the ball, two or three Highfield players swarmed around him every time. More than ever, it was up to Todd to score.

At halftime, as the players got ready to go back on the field, the voice of a Ross Corners parent rang out.

"Somebody should take a dive in the penalty box before they do!" It was Mr. Spane, who was joined by several other parents agreeing with him. "What choice do we have, when these guys do it, but the refs—"

"No, Dad." He was cut off by his son, Jerry, who said, "They cheat, Dad, we don't."

That quieted everyone down. Coach Godwin patted Jerry on the shoulder. Todd was impressed. He felt more determined than ever. He had to make the difference. He wanted to score, and he had to concentrate. He stepped on the field, feeling at last like he could do it.

Highfield dominated this time. They knew how to use their defenders for back passes. They had the ball most of the time. The Ross Corners players were wearing down, trying to break up those short passes. No goals would mean Highfield would be the champs.

"That's it, that's it!" Coach Jaynes yelled again and again. "Make 'em chase for it!"

The Ross Corners players did just that, but without much success. Then Coach Godwin told Todd to stay with their central defender, Rudy.

"He's their target man for back passes," he said. "Stay with him and break up those passes."

Todd battled Rudy with all he had. He was making things harder for Rudy, but the Highfield players knew their short passing game very well. They seemed to be playing for a tie.

Time was running out, and Todd was burning out. But he gave one last effort as a ball came back to Rudy. Todd just got a foot in and the ball sprang loose. From out of nowhere, Giorgio raced through.

He got the ball and headed for goal. Todd followed, and so did the whole Highfield team. Jaynes was howling, "Get him!" Will was ready to take on Giorgio one-on-one.

"Get him!" Jaynes shrieked.

Rudy got there with a tremendous defensive play. He blocked Giorgio's rush to goal, bouncing the ball free. Rudy and Giorgio fought for it. Todd came up and called to Giorgio, who flicked it forward. Will was off his line. Todd had the ball, far-right corner open.

Todd watched as he fell. Impossible to save this time. The ball was up and away.

So was Will, as if he knew—knew where it was going.

Fingertips again. Unbelievable. He saved it!

Even before Todd could get to his feet, the whistle blew for the end of the game. Highfield went wild. Todd just lay there, trying to catch his breath, trying to understand what had happened.

"See you in the sectional tournament, dude." Will pulled Todd to his feet. "Probably you and us in the finals."

And the winner of the section would go on to the state championship.

"How'd you do that?" Todd asked. "How'd you make that save, man?"

"See you this weekend," Will said, reminding him they had plans to meet at the Benson greenhouse, where there was a sale of pumpkins and autumn flowers. "I'll even let you in on a secret—or maybe two."

Todd was so numb that he didn't even look around for Melanie. He was miserable enough right now.

CHAPTER TEN

Shoot-out

It was a chilly, sunny Saturday morning when Will came to the Benson greenhouse. Todd had finished his work, so they went out to the bench by the stream to talk about soccer—or so Todd thought.

The conversation started out that way. Will said he had several college scouts in touch with him. No scholarships were on the table yet. His first choice had not come through.

"If you win the section," Todd said, "then get the state title, you'll be golden, man."

"Just gotta get past you, Pelé."

"Right," Todd replied, faking confidence. "You can't always be lucky."

"It's not luck, dude. It's knowledge. Of you."

Will grinned, looking at his watch. Todd tried to change the subject. He didn't want to discuss how he seemed to be choking every time he played Highfield. Will was not about to let it go, though.

"Yep, I got your number, bro."

"How so? Not just luck?" Todd asked, curious.

"You always look up just before you go for that lofted shot."

"I do?"

"Every time you loft the ball into a corner." Will looked at his watch again. "So I know what you're going to do, where the ball's going, and then I don't need luck."

Todd couldn't understand why Will would give his secret to him.

"Why are you telling me this, man?"

"Well, because I made the blunder of telling Gates how I knew where that shot was going," Will said. "Gates sneered I couldn't save that shot any other way."

"And you said you could."

"I did." Will chuckled. "And Gates said to me, 'Ferther, I'll bet you—'"

"What did you say—I mean, you said he said *ferther?*"

"That he did, and I even told the chump to spell it for me—he did, f . . . e . . . r . . . "

Todd tried to understand all this, but Will interrupted his thinking.

"Somebody here to see you, dude."

"Sorry I'm late."

Todd turned, amazed to see Melanie appear. She looked nervous and troubled. He stood up, and she suddenly put her arms around him, saying she was so sorry. Will was grinning wide, Melanie looked embarrassed, and Todd's head was spinning. He asked what was going on.

"Will found out that Gates had access to my e-mail account," Melanie began. "When he and Rudy were using my laptop. . . ."

"Only Gates could manage to spell *further* as *ferther*," Will said. "As I pointed out to him."

Gates was behind all the trouble. He'd written the unpleasant e-mails to both Melanie and Todd, pretending that they were writing to each other.

He had also taken Todd's cell phone from the locker room a few times. He quickly sent rude text messages to Melanie and put it back before Todd came in the locker room after practice. Even Rudy didn't know his friend was being a cyberbully. Rudy was furious when he found out, which made Gates all the more willing to spill the beans.

"I was so hurt," Melanie said. "I thought you didn't care—"

"Me, too. I thought you didn't."

"This," said Will, raising his elbows and one knee, "is where I exit, stage right, to allow you sweet young things to make up."

Will shuffled off, and Todd and Melanie did make up. By the time they'd talked everything over, Melanie even agreed to go to the prom with him when they were juniors—both proms, at Highfield and Ross Corners. Todd didn't know how he asked her, or whether she asked him. But it sure made him feel great.

Of course, one big distraction remained. Todd had to figure out how to take that lofted shot without looking up and signaling Will where it was going. It was the only way to beat him.

✧✧✧✧

Ross Corners went through the sectional playoffs with flying colors, winning all three games. So did Highfield, which everybody had expected. They faced each other in the fourth game for the sectional championship. The winner would go on to the state tournament.

Everyone Todd knew was at the game, which was played in a college stadium. There must have been three thousand people in the stands because this was the second game of a doubleheader—the first game was for third place in the section.

This was a night game, with the white lights making the ball shine so it could be seen spinning in the air. The atmosphere was charged with excitement. As he jogged onto the field with his teammates, Todd felt like all those eyes were on him. When the Ross Corners fans roared for the team, Todd knew he didn't want to be anywhere else in the world just then.

As they kicked the ball around in warm-ups, Giorgio played him a long ball that skipped past and toward the Highfield players. Todd saw Gates on the field and smiled broadly at him. Taken by surprise, Gates quickly turned away.

Soon, both teams got in position to start the game. Todd's heart pounded. He thought he heard his father's voice from the crowd, even Betsy's. The whistle blew. The ball was moving, with Highfield taking the kickoff.

It was a crazy start to the game. In the first five minutes, Ross Corners didn't touch the ball. In a well-drilled sequence of passes, the ball came back from the Highfield forwards, then over to Rudy. The ball went back out to the wings and then back to Rudy. It was a display of terrific teamwork until Rudy surprised Todd's entire team. Instead of a close pass, he suddenly chipped the ball to a breaking forward. The striker scored easily. At least it wasn't Gates getting the glory, Todd thought glumly.

Right then, Coach Godwin put a player on Rudy to keep him from getting the passbacks. That way, Highfield wouldn't be able to control the ball as well.

"If they don't have that backpass to Rudy," Coach Godwin said to Todd from the sideline, "their players won't have so much time to think."

Coach Godwin left Todd to play freely up front. The Ross Corners strategy worked well. Highfield still controlled the ball, but couldn't get their attack going. Rudy was tough and very good, but it frustrated him to be challenged for every ball passed back to him.

Neither team's forwards got much of the ball. The game was between Giorgio and the Highfield midfielders. As it went on, with the score still 1–0, Todd could feel the Highfield players losing confidence. The Ross Corners guys were, instead, gaining confidence.

Coach Jaynes was furious. He never sat down once and must have emptied a six-pack of water bottles. He was so frustrated that he even yanked Gates off the field to scold him. Gates was playing like he had lead in his legs. Jaynes sent Gates back on, but he was embarrassed.

Then, with the clock running out, the first real chance came for Ross Corners. Giorgio stole the ball and sprang Todd free with a slick, curling lead pass. At last, Todd was breaking away, Rudy right behind him, trying to get between him and the goal.

Todd avoided looking up at Will. Instead, he sensed where Will was positioned. Todd was at the penalty box, Rudy battling alongside him, shoulder to shoulder. Rudy used his power to throw Todd off balance, stopping the breakaway. Todd kept control of the ball, but Rudy was all over him.

"Go down!" That was Mr. Spane's voice, and it rose into a shriek. "Go down in the box, man!"

Todd was, indeed, in the penalty box, protecting the ball and dribbling. Rudy was on one side, Gates on the other. If Todd took a dive here, he might get a penalty kick. In fact, they bumped him hard, and he staggered. He stumbled, but fought to keep his feet. He wouldn't go down easy. In the next second, he saw both Rudy and Gates were down, sprawling. They had collided, and the ball was still at his feet.

Rudy quickly got back up. Todd stopped and faked a shot. Rudy threw out a leg. But Todd pulled the ball back, and pushed it across to

Giorgio, who beat two defenders and moved into the middle, looking for a shot.

"Get him! Get him!" Gates, Rudy, and Jaynes were all screaming.

Will came out for Giorgio. Will's eyes were fixed to the ball at Giorgio's feet. Will took two quick steps forward.

Todd moved into the open. Then the ball was at his feet, unexpectedly. It was another perfect pass from Giorgio. Todd was at the left of the goal, on the edge of the penalty box. He didn't look up.

Instead, he shouted, "Giorgio, go!" and faked as if he were going to pass into the middle.

In the next instant, the ball was sailing high. Everybody was frozen, watching.

All but Will, who was scrambling, leaping desperately, pawing at air. Another magnificent effort!

But the ball dropped into the far upper corner, tying the game. Will was on his back. Gates and Rudy were yelling at each other. Coach Jaynes was red faced, slumped on his chair, unable to speak. Or drink water.

Todd trotted back to the roar of the crowd and praise of his teammates. He didn't think Will would appreciate any joking just then. And scoring on him didn't feel so bad after all.

Regular time soon ended and the teams went into overtime, with Highfield back on their heels. They wanted to hold on and go to penalty kicks. Will surely could win it for them in a penalty shoot-out. But it still was very upsetting for Coach Jaynes. He was being bested by what used to be the doormat of the league. The unstoppable Highfield was struggling for a draw!

Jaynes was again screaming and insulting his players. Meanwhile, Coach Godwin was beaming, saying little. For the first time in many years, it was the Highfield defensive play that mattered, not their offense. Still, they were good at defense, and the overtime also ended in a draw.

Mighty Highfield got its wish for penalties.

In the shoot-out, each team had five penalty shots, alternating with one another. It was just the goalie and the shooter, one kick, no rebounds allowed. The crowd hushed as Giorgio took the first penalty. He ripped it low into a corner. Will had no chance.

Then Rudy scored. Jerry was next, and he hit it well, but Will made the save. Gates ballooned the ball over the crossbar.

Todd came next. He'd never been so nervous. He teed up the ball and looked at Will, who grinned, as expected. Todd took a long run as if to hammer it. Will started to go. Then Todd side-footed the ball the other way. Will recovered and leaped, but too late. Ross Corners 2, Highfield 1.

Yet, there were more penalties to take, and Will was brilliant, stopping three out of five—only Giorgio and Todd scored on him. Highfield scored three times to win the shoot-out, 3–2, and the sectional championship. Jaynes and his players went wild with happiness.

Will soon found Todd, and they embraced on the field. Disappointed as he was, Todd thought it was the right result. And he knew Highfield had the better chance for the state championship.

"Highfield was the better team today, dude," Todd said, "thanks to you."

Will was actually at a loss for words, except to stammer out a "Gadzooks!"

Todd and Will walked off the field, arms over their shoulders. Fans from both teams stood and clapped slowly. No one shouted, whistled, or stomped. Mr. Spane, who usually had a loud cheer for the players, just stood and smiled, joining the applause. Even Rudy slapped Todd's shoulder. It was a moment to remember.

Highfield did go on to win the state title, and Will earned that full college scholarship. As for Ross Corners, they began a new era of soccer excellence under Coach Godwin. Led by Todd, they became Highfield's toughest opponent on the soccer field. As for Melanie, from then on she and Todd went together to all the big dances at both Highfield and Ross Corners high schools.

Read other titles in the series **A CHAMPION SPORTS STORY**

BATTING NINTH

Chad is a terrible hitter. But when a new coach arrives, things start to change. This exciting story will keep you flipping the pages as the Rangers strive for the championship trophy, and Chad learns the value of playing the game the right way.

Library Ed. ISBN 978-0-7660-3886-8
Paperback ISBN 978-1-4644-0001-8

MATTY IN THE GOAL

Matty loves soccer, but he isn't any good at it. When he volunteers to be his team's new goalie, he hopes to become an important part of the team. Follow Matty in this kickin' soccer story as he tries to go from benchwarmer to goalie superstar.

Library Ed. ISBN 978-0-7660-3877-6
Paperback ISBN 978-1-4644-0003-2

ROUNDING THIRD, HEADING HOME!

Can Jacob's Little League team, Morey's Funeral Home, really go from worst to first? You won't be able to put down this funny, action-packed story about a ragtag team going for glory when they meet their nemesis for a shot at the championship.

Library Ed. ISBN 978-0-7660-3876-9
Paperback ISBN 978-1-4644-0002-5

TONY'S LAST TOUCHDOWN

Anthony is the best linebacker in the city. On the field, he strikes fear in his opponents. Off the field, he has a lot to worry about. Follow Anthony in this gripping story about a football star who learns there are more important things in life than football.

Library Ed. ISBN 978-0-7660-3885-1
Paperback ISBN 978-1-4644-0004-9

About the Author

Stuart A.P. Murray, a native of Scotland but raised in New Jersey, has written more than forty books, including a soccer instructional for young players. He played college and semi-pro soccer and has coached youth, high school, and college teams.